Oh No, Annie!

Tony and Jan Payne

Illustrated by Rosie Reeve

Dolphin Paperbacks

First published in Great Britain in 2004
as a Dolphin Paperback
by Orion Children's Books
a division of the Orion Publishing Group Ltd
Orion House
5 Upper St Martin's Lane
London WC2H 9EA

Reprinted 2004

A catalogue record for this book is
available from the British Library

Printed in Great Britain by
Clays Ltd, St Ives plc

ISBN 1 84255 157 4

For Lee and Claudia, with love as always.
T&J P

Contents

I Bought a Moose for Granny

When the wildlife park near us closed down and they sold off the animals, I bought a moose for Granny.

I called him Tickle.

Gran tried hard not to show it, but she was really pleased, I could tell.

Gran put Tickle in the cupboard under the stairs at first, but he didn't really fit, so we gave him her spare room. He liked it in there, but ate a rubber plant and the handles off a cupboard, so Granny said he had to go out in the garden.

I don't think pets should have to go out in the cold and wet. It's not fair.

Anyway, Granny asked me if I'd walk the moose for her as her legs are not what they

were. But I'm much too busy to walk a moose and Gran has lots of time when she's not making jam or anything. I think she's just being lazy. Also, I think her legs *are* what they were because I've looked and they're the same.

Granny took the moose down to the post office to get her pension and to the super-market for some taramasalata, but they wouldn't let her in, so she had to tie Tickle to a tree outside. When she came out, the moose had pulled up the tree and run away. There were bits of tree all up the high street, but no sign of Tickle.

Granny pretended to be glad – to save my feelings I expect – skipping about and flapping her arms up and down and yodelling as she swung round in the store's revolving doors, but she didn't fool me. She was really sad, I could tell.

I went back to the wildlife park to get

something else to cheer her up, but they didn't have much left. I really wanted an Australian wombat, but they'd run out. Pity – I like wombats. In the end I got a giant tortoise and a pangolin, which is not a musical instrument by the way, it's an animal. It looks like a big fir cone with a long nose. I reckoned the tortoise and pangolin together made up one moose-worth.

Granny put on her pretend-exasperation look when I gave them to her and rolled her eyes the way grannies do.

The giant tortoise was all right – but she didn't have a lot of energy. Once she'd eaten everything green in the garden, finishing with the rhubarb

(which, OK, is mainly pink), she didn't move
again for a week. Plus, she was a bit brown –
and so was the garden by then – and you
tripped over her if you were not careful, due
to not seeing her.

Actually, she was a bit boring really.

The pangolin was sweet, though, and
had a lot of personality, except he stuck
his tongue in your ear and wiggled it
about. Gran sent me to the library in the
high street to look up what they have for
dinner.

"Where am I going to find enough *ants* in
Sebastapol Street?" she asked when I got

back – quite loudly, actually. She must have been *really* interested.

I went to the park to get a kilo of ants but they wouldn't stay in the bag. I brought some back on the outside of the bag and all up my arms, but most of them stayed on the bus when I got off. There weren't really enough ants left for a whole lunch then and I had to give the pangolin my M&Ms.

Next day I met Jessica Jolly who lives in the same road as me. She'd been to the wildlife park sale too and bought stuff. We did a swap. My pangolin for her komodo dragon. Her mum is allergic to komodo

dragons, she said. I took him back to Gran's on a lead. I don't think he was a real dragon, actually, because he didn't seem to breathe out smoke much … or fly … but he's really lovely and fits perfectly in the bath, except for his tail.

And his head.

And his legs, which stick out over the sides.

 Jessica said that komodo dragons only seem to eat once a month, so Gran has plenty of time to find out what he  likes. Gran was really pleased with me and my kindness, I could tell.

But then the komodo dragon disappeared! He must have been able to fly after all because the window was open and the bathroom is at the top of the house. He couldn't have just jumped. He left something smelly in the bath too and Granny said she couldn't take much more of this. Excitement, I suppose she meant.

The giant tortoise was looking really drab and people were still tripping over her, so I brightened her up with some paint I found in the cupboard at home. It didn't actually

mention tortoises on the tin, but I'm pretty
sure it's all right, there's no poison lead in it
or anything. I painted each bump on her
shell with a different pattern – flowers plus
zigzags and stripes and other stuff and all in
different colours. She looked really nice –
just like a patchwork quilt, Jessica said –
whatever that is.

Now the tortoise was so colourful she
brightened up the whole garden and no one
tripped over her. But she still didn't do much.

In fact, whenever I saw her shell, I wondered if there was anyone in. She must have thumped about when I wasn't looking, though, because she bashed a hole in the fence and went next door. It hardly seemed worth the effort of getting her back again because she was just as interesting on the other side of the fence and, anyway, old Mister Kravitz has bad eyesight and so he won't miss his chrysanthamums.

I went to the wildlife park *yet again*. It was so disappointing – the shelves were empty and the man in the office said almost everything had gone. Only small animals were left, he said.

Well, I didn't want my gift to Granny to be *less* than a moose or a giant tortoise and a pangolin or a komodo dragon, so I guessed what a moose would weigh and asked the man if I could have about a tonne of mixed small animals.

He just laughed and said he didn't have that many and I would have to make do with three and a half kilos. Well ... you don't get many animals for three and a half kilos, that's for sure.

Not a mooseworth, anyway.

I think there were about two dozen animals altogether. I thought he said the one looking like a lizard was a comedian, which

was good because Gran says
she likes a good joke. It was a
'chameleon', though,
and the man wrote
it down so I didn't
forget.

The new animals
loved it at
Granny's, but I
had to put them
all in different
rooms so they
didn't eat each
other. It was
getting really nice
and interesting in
the house. It was a
bit whiffy though
and Gran stayed in
the kitchen all the
time now with a
bottle of her home-
made wine. To
celebrate, probably.

She was always asking where the chameleon was. Once I told her I thought it was in disguise on the curtains in the front room. Gran said that was silly – she said the chameleon might be very good at changing colour, but it didn't do chintz. I think that was a funny remark, but I didn't understand it.

Gran said old Mister Kravitz next door had had the council round telling him off for leaving his old patchwork quilt out in the garden. Poor Mister Kravitz.

I had a look and they didn't know what they were talking about. There wasn't *anything* in his garden – except the tortoise I painted, of course.

Then Granny had some really good luck! She went to put some sheets in the airing cupboard and the komodo dragon fell out. It had been there in the warm all the time.

The day after that, the giant tortoise returned from next door because she'd run out of chrysanthamums to eat and then Tickle turned up in the middle of the night

with another moose friend he'd found
somewhere.

If that wasn't enough good news, Jessica
Jolly brought the pangolin back. Her mother
was allergic to pangolins too. Also, she didn't
like pangolin spit in her ear.

Gran wasn't home next morning when I
called in on my way to school. There was a

note from her saying she'd
been called away for an
emergency holiday in
Australia.

Granny can't fool me.
She hasn't gone to Australia for an
emergency holiday at all. She wants to pay
me back for all my thoughtfulness, I can tell.

Granny's gone to get me a wombat!

My School and Other Things I Don't Like

I've got to go to school, I *know*.
But I don't want to. I'd rather
be somewhere else. Why can't I
be with Mum this week,
climbing up Ben Nevis?
(Ben Nevis is a
mountain in Scotland.
It's not a person.)
My school is in
Glendale Close,
right next door to
Bath Road, where

27

I live. It only takes five minutes
to get there, except I usually
hop or walk backwards, so
it takes a bit longer. I like
going to school, I
just don't like
school.

Our
teacher is
Miss Felton.
She's very
strong. She has
a moustache and wears
trousers that look itchy and
like they've been made from sacks.

I like writing – but not in class. I do it for
myself.

I'm FED UP with making useless things
out of toilet roll tubes and painting them and
sticking them to the windows. Also it must be
really unhygienic. Jessica Jolly says a lot of
toilet paper is recycled. That means it's used
again, doesn't it? It's disgusting.

This morning we weighed some beans and

added some
beans and
took away
some beans
and worked out
the weight of one
bean. So *that's*
what a bean
weighs …
Amazing … I
don't think!

  At morning break I
sat next to Lizzie Alexander and Tomas
Flem. Lizzie's nose looks like it's been hit with
a brick. Tomas is very thin and
his skin is white with pink
blotches. He looks like
a rasher of
bacon. I don't
like both of
them. At
the next
table were
John and

Ron, the Tubman twins,
and Roy Pawson. I don't
like them too. I also don't
like anyone else,
except Jessica Jolly
who I only don't
like sometimes.

Before we
had our lunch,
we learned about
'the life-cycle of a
peanut', but I looked out of the window
instead. There was a wall outside and it was
much more interesting.

Then we were given a project to do at
home. We had to grow a
vegetable from seed and
look what happened
and then write
about it.

BOR ... RING!
Miss Felton
could just *tell* us
what happens, we

don't need to *see* it happen. Also, Dad has a vegetable garden at home. I can ask *him* if I ever need to know how a vegetable grows (which is *never*). Teacher gave us some vegetable seeds.

There were lots of different sorts and I got peas.

"Dad," I said, when I got home, "I've got a special project to do and you have to dig some dirt for me ... And plant some peas ... And then tell me what happens, in three hundred words."

"That sounds like *my* project, then," said Dad. "Do I have to hand it in for you too?"

He wouldn't do it for me! He said he wanted to work on something in our front room while Mum is out of the way. He's making a model of New York out of carrots.

The ground in our garden is hard and the dirt is so ... dirty! No way was I digging that. But I was lucky. I found some plastic bags full of really soft, black dirt in Dad's greenhouse. There was a row of them all along one side. They had 'Tomato Gro-bag' on them. I had peas, not tomatoes, but I didn't think the bag would know the difference. Anyway, I pulled out some plants that were already growing in the bag and poked my peas in and stood well back.

Then I waited.

I had my trombone lesson at seven and it was nearly that *already* ... so the peas had better not be long.

I waited *over half an hour.* Then I had to go to Mr. Corolli's for my lesson and when I came back there was *still* nothing growing.

What a total waste of time!

Well, I

33

thought, I'm going back in. I can't hang around waiting for peas to grow. I've got things to do.

Next morning there was still nothing growing. At school Miss Felton asked if anybody had anything to report about our seeds.

Only two of us put up our hands. Me and Billy Williams. My peas must have died, but I wasn't going to tell anyone. Miss Felton would think I killed them.

"Billy," Miss Felton said, "what have you grown?"

"Mustard and cress, Miss," Billy said, looking dead smug.

"And how did you grow them?"

"I grew them on a wet flannel."

Roy Pawson called out, "That's why he's got a dirty face, Miss!"

I didn't laugh like the others because I haven't got a sense of humour.

"Be quiet, Roy," snapped Miss Felton. "That's very good, Billy. And what did you grow, Ann?"

"Peas," I said.

35

"And they've grown?" She looked really surprised and her eyebrows went right up under her fringe and stayed there. "Tell us about them."

"Well . . . These plants shot up," I said. "Green ones . . . With all leaves and stuff."

"Yes?" Miss Felton said, like she wanted more.

"And, um . . . they're quite tall. About as tall as me."

"That's extraordinary in only one day, Ann. Are there peas on these plants?"

"Oh, yes, lots of peas," I said. "*All over* the branches."

"Would that be the branches of the pea . . . er . . . *bush*?"

"More like a tree, Miss," I said.

Miss Felton wanted me to come to the front of the class and she stood behind me with her hands on my shoulders.

"It's not every day in Glendale Primary that we have someone who has actually grown a pea tree," she said. "And, amazingly, in less than twenty-four hours. Before I

36

contact the Guinness Book of Records, let's give Ann a big round of applause."

Well . . . I don't often get praised in class. I actually smiled . . . and I never smile.

"You don't understand sarcasm, do you, Ann?" Miss Felton said.

"No, Miss," I said back. And I didn't.

Miss Felton told me I could stay behind after school and read about peas. She said that was what I richly deserved.

It didn't seem much of a prize. But it was the only one that Miss Felton gave to anyone – and *I* got it! It's weird though – normally you stay behind after school as a *punishment*, not when you've done something really good and got applauded.

I didn't mind really. There was nothing happening at home. Mum was off on one

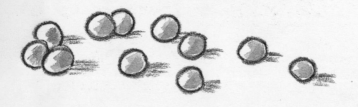

of her adventures and Dad was carving carrots into skyscrapers. I couldn't go to Gran's either, it was darts' night at her pub. So I had an extra hour at school, reading about peas, and then I went home.

One day, *months* later, Dad said, "How come there are lots of peas growing in the greenhouse? I didn't plant any peas."

I ran out to look. There were plants growing out of my tomato bag. They didn't look much like trees really,

gro-bag

but they *were*
as tall as me
and, d'you know
what? The peas were
already packed in *tubes*, like
sweets. They hung down from the
stem and when you pressed the zip at
the side, the tubes opened – and *real*
peas fell out.

My peas that I grew all on my own!

I got really excited. One
tube had fourteen
peas in it!

I weighed them
and measured them
with a ruler and
added some and took
some away and worked
out what a single pea
weighed. Then I found out
how to cook them and I
made pea soup.

It was atrocious.

But really interesting.

A lot more
interesting than
school.

Annie's Birthday Surprise Carrot Pudding

On Tuesday I had to go to the laundrette.

Honestly, I've got better things to do with my time. I've plans of my own to make the world a better place – and they don't include going to the laundrette.

It all started with Gran saying old Mister Kravitz was having his brothers over from Poland, because it's his birthday, and he didn't know how he'd feed them all.

I'm a very thoughtful person. I thought I'd

make them something dead good to eat so they'd remember their stay in our country. The only thing I've actually made before is Christmas pudding. Mum showed me how ages ago, although she's not the best cook in the world.

"You can use almost anything in the cupboard to make a Christmas pudding," she said. "There's loads of ingredients and it doesn't matter if you haven't got all of them."

So I decided to make a *birthday* pudding.

I made up a recipe all by myself. I looked in the cupboard. Flour – got some of that. Suet – packet in the fridge. Sugar, yes. Sultanas, currants, raisins, mixed peel, nuts, hmmm, hmmm, dum-di-dum . . . No, none of those.

I used carrots instead. I called it Annie's Birthday Surprise Carrot Pudding. Dad likes growing things, but he grows mainly carrots. I was doing him a favour using them up.

Dad was in the garden now, digging up some more. Mum was out, so he was supposed to be looking after me, but he's useless at that.

I made an enormous lot of pudding mixture because people from other countries don't get enough to eat. Mixing it all up was really hard because

there was so much of it and we didn't have enough bowls. All right, maybe I shouldn't have used the washing machine, but now it doesn't work, OK, and that's why I have to go to the laundrette.

Pity really. The mixture looked great going round and round in the little window – until it was too smeared up to see through.

Mum came back and, when she saw it, said to go and clean my room. She just says things like that to get rid of me so she can do

her calming down breathing exercises. I have to clean my room a lot.

The man from the shop had to come and open the door with an electric drill . . .

And a screwdriver.

And a hammer and chisel.

I think I used too much suet.

Mum couldn't go to the laundrette because she was running in the Paris marathon later on. I expect she was really sorry she couldn't take my dirty clothes

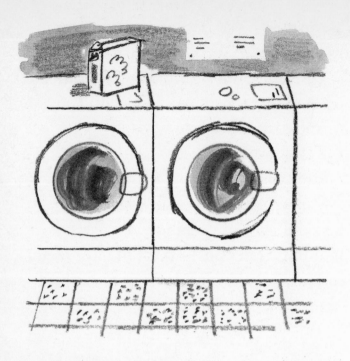

herself. Dad said I would have to go and do
the washing instead.

There was one megalot of stuff. I put it all
into bin-liners and put the bin-liners into a
wheelbarrow and heaved that all the way up
the high street. Nobody uses the laundrette
much on a Tuesday and that was great. I
didn't want anyone seeing me do the
washing!

I fished out all the white things, like Mum

does, because the colour comes out of
the coloured stuff and spoils everything. I
filled up one machine with the whites and
poured a packet of soapflakes in, shoved in
some money and pushed the starting-up
button.

There was no way I could separate the
other clothes, though. Every one was a
different colour ... Well, every two really
because they were nearly all socks. I couldn't

be bothered to pick out the pairs, they were too mixed up. There were loads of machines, though, so I put one sock in each, started them up and then I was rushing around opening and closing doors, scooping out one clean sock and putting a dirty one in, pouring soap and adding coins. It took for ever!

When I got back, Mum had gone off to Paris and the machine repairing man had gone too, but he'd rescued all my pudding mixture. There were pots of goo all over the place.

You have to put the glop into squares of cloth, tie them up and boil them to make puddings. I couldn't find any cloth to use, but it didn't matter. I had the socks.

Things turned out really well! The colours of the socks had run, so I ended up with forty-eight, striped, red and green and blue and purple, sock-shaped birthday puddings. They looked like freaky wellies. I couldn't find any decorations or candles, so I sprayed some carrots with gold paint and put glitter on a few conkers. They looked brilliant.

I couldn't wait to meet old Mister Kravitz's hungry family and see their looks of gratitude. And that made me think of Gran, who lives next door to Mister Kravitz. I hadn't been round for a few days and if I didn't drag her out sometimes, she'd just stay at home

making chutney. Anyway, I needed help
carrying the puddings.

"What, with my back?" she said, when I
asked her.

"Of course with your back."

She looked horrified. "The puddings are
so heavy!"

"Naturally they're heavy," I said. "They're
full of stuff! I bet they're twice as heavy as
the puddings at Sainsbury's."

So that was the second time that day Dad's
barrow came in handy.

When we got to number 24, Mister Kravitz
was overjoyed to see us and when we said
there was another barrowload of Birthday
Surprise Carrot Pudding, he asked five of his
brothers to go back with me. Gran stayed by
the drinks' cupboard.

We went back to Bath Road. One of
the Mister Kravitzes spoke some English
and he said they were a sort of circus family,
which probably explained why they were
doing somersaults all along Cranberry
Close.

When we got to the house,
the Mister Kravitzes took four puddings
each and there was one left over,
which I left behind for Beckham,
my gerbil.

It was harder talking to
the men on the way back
because they were standing on
each other's shoulders
and the top Mister
Kravitz was a
long way up. I
had to
shout.

I told
them all
about my morning in the laundrette and they told me all about Poland.

Well – I think it was about Poland, but it
was in Polish and I didn't understand a lot,
but their pudding juggling was amazing.
They didn't drop even one pudding when
the bottom Mister Kravitz walked into the
wall of McDonald's by mistake and the

others fell off when they hit the sign over the door.

When we got back to old Mister Kravitz's, we were invited in for the birthday party. I thought of the boring old meal we'd get back home, with carrot salad and carrot cake and probably carrot ice cream. (Dad was cooking.)

Gran said yes before I did.

Gran found some of the Mister Kravitzes in the dining room. Five minutes later she was being thrown upside down on someone's head and HEY-YUPing like she was having a really good time and was a real circus acrobat. Especially after she put on the leotard. There must have been another ten Mister Kravitzes in the other room. They were making a human pyramid on the coffee table.

Gran went back next door to get her double bass and her xylophone because she wanted to play for everyone. You wouldn't think you could play a double bass and a

HAPPY

xylophone at the same time, would you? But she nearly did it and then she tried to write 'Happy Birthday' all around the room with crazyfoam. But she'd been at the cooking sherry by then and was getting over-excited, so some of the letters were the wrong way round or upside

down, but all the Mister Kravitzes thought it was hilarious because she'd accidently written 'BUM' on the windows in Polish.

Later we ate loads of strange food, but they all said that my Birthday Surprise Carrot Pudding was the strangest. I bet it was the best thing they'd ever eaten. They said it tasted exactly like something they get in Poland, made from prune yoghurt, potato peelings and

dripping. Wasn't that a nice thing to say?

I didn't want to go home afterwards . . . that's because at home I had 48, dirty pudding-socks to wash.

On Friday I had to go to the laundrette.

PRIZE IDIOTS

In November the newspaper had a children's photo competition.

We had to take a picture of a beauty spot – except I didn't know what a beauty spot was then. I took a photo of the pimple on Jessica Jolly's nose. Not just a pimple actually, there was a blackhead and a mole and some other stuff. The photo was taken close up. You couldn't see Jessica's face – her spots filled the whole picture. Purple and brown they were. Red and orange . . . and green. Really colourful. The newspaper thought I'd taken a picture of mountains in autumn.

I won first prize ... *Except* ...

I didn't *want* first prize.

I wanted second prize, so I told everyone that Billy Williams's photo was better than mine, even though it wasn't and his ears stick out. The paper still said mine was best. So *he* came second and won a trip to Kid's World in Florida and I won a trip to *Iceland*!

OK, it was a free holiday, but it wasn't

Kid's World, was it? And Ice-land sounds cold. Still, part of the prize was that they gave me this really neat camera to take. I had to make a sort of photo diary of my trip and the photos would be printed in the *Weekly News*. Pity Jessica Jolly wasn't around – there might be other parts of her face that I could photograph instead of going all the way to Iceland and getting turned into an icicle to take them.

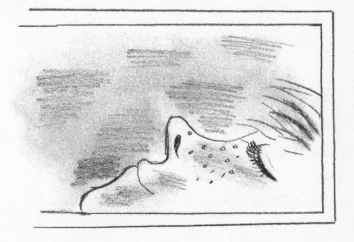

I won two tickets and I had to go with a responsible adult. But I don't *know* any responsible adults. Anyway, Mum was

driving a lorry of food aid to Africa. Dad was doing something important in the garden. That only left Gran. She said she'd come with me and *pretend* to be responsible.

Gran spent a whole day getting warm clothes from the charity shop. By the time we had to go to the airport, there was this huge pile of stuff filling her hallway. She only has one case, so she put most of the clothes *on*, including a knitted teapot cosy she'd bought by mistake and was wearing pulled down over her ears. Then there was no Granny showing at all, just a nose sticking through the tea-cosy hole. I could have *rolled* her to the car, she was so round. I took a photo of her.

When we got to the airport desk, the man said I had too much baggage and I said that's my Granny and so he let us get on the plane. Inside the plane, a woman in a

uniform said Gran had to go under the seat in front of me or in the locker – until she heard Gran saying *no way* in a muffled voice and realised she was a person and not luggage.

In Iceland it *was* cold – there was snow and everything. The town we stayed in was weird. All the houses looked like big tin sheds. They

were made of wavy metal sheets nailed
together and painted in bright colours, so
from up above they looked like Lego.

We got to the hotel (red and blue Lego)
and put our clothes away. After we'd filled up
the cupboards, Gran still looked like a full
laundry basket, with all the layers she was
wearing. When we'd finished, we went to the

dining room for something
to eat. We looked at the
menu, but it was written in
Icelandish.

"What's this then?" Gran asked
the waiter, pointing to something.

The man looked over
Gran's shoulder.
"Faloloppy-
falloloppa,"
he said, or
something like
that. "It's fish
that's been buried
in dirt for six
months."

"You've got to
be kidding!" said
Gran. "What's this one?"

"Eggs . . . but only buried in
dirt for *three* months."

Gran's face was getting longer
and longer. She covered her eyes
with one hand and pointed at

something on the menu with the other without looking. "And this?"

"That is sheep's head that's been buried —"

"Hold it!" said Gran, holding up a hand. "Listen, have you got *anything* that has never, ever, been buried in dirt? Something a bit more like food?"

"Of course," said the man.

"Then we'll have two cheese and pickle sandwiches and a nice cup of tea," she said.

Next morning, Gran decided she wanted to swim in the 'Blue Lagoon', which is supposed to be really famous in Iceland. That sounded all right, until we got there. It wasn't a swimming pool, like I was expecting. It was a *lake,* out in the open doors. In November!

The man said, "You'll be OK, the water's hot." But the changing shed wasn't and I had to run through the snow and jump in before I froze to death. The water smelled like used fireworks. It was weird because my face was really cold and, under the water, I was being cooked pink. I kept near the edge and swam

and it was nice ... like swimming in soup, but
the edge was sharp rocks, not tiles, and that's
all there was to hang on to. I was hot now, so
I got out and went to get the camera for my
Weekly News job.

A door crashed open and Gran shot out of
the changing shed, running faster than I'd
ever seen her move in my life. She yelled
GERONIMO! And jumped into the water
in her underwear, pinching her nose with
one hand and holding her knickers up with
the other. I got a good photo of her. The
newspaper would like that one.

I took another good one of Granny smearing her face with mud from the bottom of the pool. "The brochure says it will make me beautiful," she said. "What d'you think?"

"It doesn't work," I told her. Her face still looked like a pepperoni pizza. Sort of red and lumpy. Very photogenic though.

The next day we went to see *Geysir*.
"This is the most famous geyser in the

world," Gran said, reading from her guide book. "All the other geysers in the world are named after it."

Great! But I didn't know what a geyser was. It looked like a hole in the ground. Gran said it used to spout boiling water miles up in the air at exactly the same times every day and was really spectacular, until people found out that throwing washing powder in made it spout up straight away. Now Geysir is all mixed up. Its clock doesn't work any more.

I thought about Billy Williams riding the Dipper of Death in Florida, where you go up *ten miles* and loop the loop at a *thousand* miles an hour. And I had a hole in the ground to look at. And even that was out of order.

I *didn't* take a photograph.

I should have known Gran was up to something when she said she wanted to see Geysir *again* next day. I mean, there's just rocks there and more rocks. And a hole. No shops or amusements or camel rides or anything.

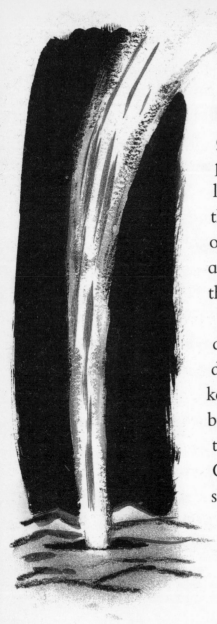

When
we got there,
Granny opened
a bag and I
thought we were
going to have our
picnic, but she
looked around and
then took a packet
of soap powder out
and threw it down
the hole!

A scary rumble
came from deep
down, like a million
kettles coming to the
boil. I ran away from
the edge. So did
Gran, but not before
she'd thrown in her
washing too!

She just can't
stand wasting
hot water.

There was an
enormous *whoosh*
and this huge water
jet went shooting up
a hundred miles into
the sky, blowing
bubbles. Granny's
clothes rose up too,
did a twirl at the top,
and went back down
into the hole again. While
we were watching, a busload of people
turned up and they started cheering when
there was a specially good display of
washing. "This is almost interesting," I
thought.

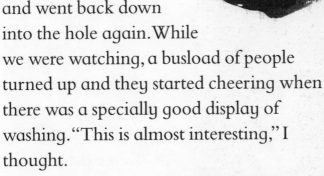

We caught some clothes as they were
thrown out. The trick was to catch
everything before it hit the ground. The bus
people ran
about catching
stuff too, but
some clothes
didn't get out

of Geysir at all. I expect they're still going up and down in the waterspout three times

a day and making people laugh.

Gran lost a big pair of frilly knickers because they got caught on a telephone wire a mile away. I bet the people who go to see Geysir now are still trying to work that one out. I took a photograph of course.

★

The time seemed to whizz by. We went out in a boat with whales and dolphins. We saw a volcano spitting red-hot lava. We found all sorts of interesting stuff and I took photos of everything. I threw away the scenery ones, though. I wanted to capture Gran instead – the real Granny. I wanted to see her look of gratitude when she saw photographs of just herself, splashed large across the newspaper's front page.

And then the holiday was over and we had to come home.

Gran left most of her clothes behind as a gift to the people of Iceland. "They smelled of rotten eggs anyway," she said.

At the airport we met Billy Williams coming back from Kid's World. He said

half the attractions
had been closed, it had
rained and he'd had food
poisoning for four
days.

And he was on
crutches with his
leg in plaster.

That was the photograph I liked best!

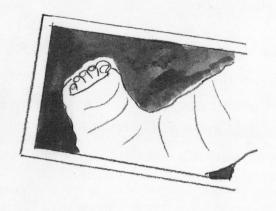

*Watch out for the next amazing
'Annie' book, which is coming soon:*

Not Again, Annie!

Four more fantastic stories
following Annie's fun adventures

*Watch out for the next amazing
'Annie' book, which is coming soon:*

Oh No, Annie – Again!

Four more fantastic stories
following Annie's fun adventures